The Edelweiss Pirates

The image in this book is used with the permission of: World History Archive/
Alamy Stock Photo, p. 32.

KAR-BEN PUBLISHING, INC.
A division of Lerner Publishing Group, Inc.
241 First Avenue North
Minneapolis, MN 55401 USA
1-800-4-KARBEN
Website address: www.karben.com

Main body text set in Breughel Com 15/20.
Typeface provided by Linotype.

Library of Congress Cataloging-in-Publication Data

Names: Elvgren, Jennifer Riesmeyer, author. | Stamatiadi, Daniela, illustrator.
Title: The Edelweiss pirates / by Jennifer Elvgren ; illustrated by Daniela
    Stamatiadi.
Description: Minneapolis : Kar-Ben Publishing, [2018] | Audience: Ages 8-12 ;
    Grades 4 to 6.
Identifiers: LCCN 2017030089| ISBN 9781512483604 (lb) | ISBN 9781512483611
    (pb) | ISBN 9781541524064 (eb pdf)
Classification: LCC PZ7.E543 Ede 2018 | DDC [Fic]—dc23

LC record available at https://lccn.loc.gov/2017030089

Manufactured in the United States of America
1-43360-33172-12/8/2017

The Edelweiss Pirates

Jennifer Elvgren

illustrations by
Daniela Stamatiadi

KAR-BEN
PUBLISHING

Plink.
Plink.
Plink.

I wake to the sound of pebbles hitting glass.
I unlock the window.

"What did you play tonight?" I ask my older brother, Albert, as he slides into our bedroom holding his clarinet case.

"Paris jazz, Louis Armstrong, Duke Ellington. Everyone Hitler hates." He takes off his jacket, his Edelweiss pin glinting on his shirt. "Usual crowd. Lots of swing dancing."

"Take me next time," I beg. "I want to be an Edelweiss Pirate."

"You know I can't, Kurt. The rotten Hitler Youth are everywhere. They beat us up for not joining them. For playing jazz. For dancing. We could be sent to jail—or to work camps. You're too young, and it's too dangerous."

Before I can protest, he presses a record into my hands.
A Louis Armstrong album! I can't wait to listen to it.

Over the weekend, I invite Fritz over to listen
to the new album. We're best friends and we both
love jazz. Since Fritz is Jewish and I'm not, he
sneaks in through our side door, hidden by hedges,
so the patrolling Hitler Youth won't notice.

We listen to the record over and over until we can both play it by ear. Fritz on his sax. Me on my trumpet.

At school, there are now portraits of Hitler in every classroom. During history class, a girl stands under Hitler and presents a project about the First World War. She says that the Jews are traitors to Germany.

Fritz stares at his desk. My face burns, and
I imagine myself playing my favorite riff from
Louis Armstrong's *Saint Louis Blues.*

Plink.
Plink.
Plink.   I let Albert in. "Who did you play tonight?"
"No music this time," Albert says. "We painted
over the swastika graffiti under the bridge. I signed
my code name nice and big."

"What's your code name?" I ask.
There's a big pause.
"It's Swing," says Albert finally. "No one can know.
You must keep this secret."
"I promise," I say. "I want to be an Edelweiss Pirate."
"No." Albert shakes his head.

At school, the math teacher makes the whole class raise their arms and say, "Heil Hitler." Everyone's arm shoots up but Fritz's. The teacher smacks his shoulder with a ruler. Fritz bites his bottom lip.

I want to say something, but I can't find any words. I sit down and hold a pencil like a pretend trumpet under my desk. I practice the fingerings to *Saint Louis Blues*.

Plink.
Plink.
Plink.

I let Albert in. "Who did you play tonight?"

"No music again," says Albert. "We were passing out anti-Hitler leaflets around the neighborhood. Tomorrow we'll deliver the rest to other towns."

"Please let me help!" I say. "I want to be an Edelweiss Pirate."

"The answer is still no," Albert replies.

"Will you be back for my band concert?" I ask.

"Of course. We'll all be there." Albert gives me a sly smile.

At school, my literature teacher calls Fritz to the front of the class and makes him read a story aloud. The story says Jews are our enemies. Fritz's voice cracks.

Our classmates are laughing. I tell the teacher I'm sick and run to the bathroom. I hum *Saint Louis Blues* until I feel calmer. I wish I could *do* something, like Albert.

At the school band concert, Mother and Father sit at the front of the auditorium. I don't see Albert.

Maestro gives the downbeat, and we start playing sad and heavy music by Richard Wagner, Hitler's favorite composer.

As we play, I think about Fritz—the history project, the ruler, the horrible book. All the times I sat there and did nothing.

My heart is heavy.

Before I know it, *Saint Louis Blues* is coming out of my trumpet.

I close my eyes and play **louder** . . .
And **louder** . . .

. . . until I've drowned out Wagner and
the rest of the band stops playing.
    I keep playing, hitting those riffs just
like Louis. The notes shimmer in the air.

I open my eyes. Mother and Father look surprised, worried. But I see some people nodding along with the beat. Fritz catches my eye and grins.

Suddenly the door at the back of the auditorium bursts open. It's Albert and the other Pirates! They dance their way down the aisles, then raise their instruments and join me in playing *Saint Louis Blues*. Albert winks at me.

Maestro grabs my ear. "You will be sorry for playing this forbidden music!"

The Pirates keep playing. As the curtains close, I see Mother and Father standing up and joining other audience members in defiant dancing.

We all make it out of the auditorium
before the Hitler Youth show up.

In the morning, I dress for school. I may be expelled today, but I don't feel one bit sorry. I pick up my jacket and something shiny catches my eye. Under the collar is an Edelweiss pin with a note attached.

My heart skips a beat.
"You're one of us now," the note says in Albert's handwriting.
"Your code name is Blues."

I am an Edelweiss Pirate.

AUTHOR'S NOTE

By 1938, open anti-Semitism became increasingly accepted throughout Germany, including in public schools. Portraits of Adolf Hitler hung in all classrooms. Students saluted Hitler at the start of class. They read books and played games that made fun of Jews. Teachers and students verbally and physically abused Jewish students.

At age fourteen, boys were expected to join the Hitler Youth and girls, the League of German Girls. But in western Germany a group of dissenters called the Edelweiss Pirates arose.

From working class backgrounds, the Pirates left school at the allowed age of fourteen to avoid joining the Hitler Youth and the League of German Girls. They were still young enough to be exempt from military service, which was required at seventeen.

Edelweiss Pirates Youth Group in Nazi Germany (1938).

The Pirates grew their hair long, wore colorful clothes, listened to jazz, swing danced, traveled, and camped in mixed groups—all forbidden activities.

Taking on code names, they resisted in other ways too. During World War II (1939–1945), they fought against Hitler Youth, created anti-Nazi graffiti, distributed anti-Nazi leaflets, sabotaged Nazi automobiles and supply trains, stole and distributed food, and helped some Jews and dissenters hide or leave the country.

Numbering more than 5,000, some of the Pirates were beaten, jailed and sent to work camps. A few were executed. In 2005, Germany officially recognized the Edelweiss Pirates as a resistance group, a tribute to those young people who dared to stand up to Nazi tyranny.